DESPICABLE ME 3: DELUXE PICTURE BOOK

A CENTUM BOOK 978-1-911460-39-8

PUBLISHED IN GREAT BRITAIN BY CENTUM BOOKS LTD

THIS EDITION PUBLISHED 2017

© 2017 UNIVERSAL STUDIOS.

1 3 5 7 9 10 8 6 4 2

CENTUM BOOKS LTD, 20 DEVON SQUARE, NEWTON ABBOT, DEVON, TQ12 2HR, UK

BOOKS@CENTUMBOOKSLTD.CO.UK

CENTUM BOOKS LIMITED REG. NO. 07641486

A CIP CATALOGUE RECORD FOR THIS BOOK IS AVAILABLE FROM THE BRITISH LIBRARY

PRINTED IN ITALY.

ILLUMINATION PRESENTS

DESPICABLE ME3™

DELUXE PICTURE BOOK

centum

STARRING

GRU

Super-villain turned super-spy.
Father to Agnes, Edith and Margo.

LUCY

Top AVL agent and mother
to Agnes, Edith and Margo.

GIRLS

Agnes, Edith and Margo –
members of Gru's Crew!

DAVE AND JERRY

Faithful and loyal to
their Master, Gru.

BALTHAZAR BRATT

80s child TV star
turned super-villain.

CLIVE THE ROBOT

Bratt's super-villain
robot sidekick.

THE DUMONT DIAMOND

LARGEST diamond in the world.

80s DICTIONARY

Some of these words are likely unfamiliar to you, but are words everyone should know (according to Balthazar Bratt).

THE ROBOT

A super-cool dance move that makes you look like a robot (and maybe a bit silly too).

KEYTAR

A musical instrument that is a cross between a guitar and keyboard. It is the preferred instrument of choice for any 80s band.

SYNTH

No 80s track is complete without some electronic string or synth sounds. Perfect music to get your mullet shaking!

MULLET

A popular haircut in the 80s, which involved growing your hair long at the back and keeping it short on the sides . . . in other words **HIDEOUS!**

SHOULDER PADS

No jacket from the 80s was complete without pointy pads on the shoulders. The pointier, the better.

FAMILY LIFE WAS NEVER DULL. Agnes had
her unwavering enthusiasm for **EVERYTHING**,
Edith loved to plot pranks and Margo . . . well,
she was going through those difficult teenage
years. Not forgetting the Minions, who still loved
fart blasters and creating their own daily mischief.

Lucy and Gru were a team and tackled the challenges of parenthood as they would any villain, working together as a team. There was **NOTHING** that anyone could do that could ruin their happy existence . . .

All was not lost, however, as Lucy had an
idea to get Gru, Dave and Jerry on board.
"GET READY!" she cried, but Gru didn't
have any time to think about what
he was waiting for . . .

. . . Lucy blasted the water and Gru, Dave and Jerry
found themselves flying through the air on a jet of water.

"GO GET HIM, GRU-GRU!"
said Lucy lovingly,
as Gru landed with a
THUMP on the deck of
the pink-bubblegum
coated ship.

The Minions overshot and missed the boat and instead landed on the beach.

"Alpha team, the diamond is secure," confirmed Gru, taking the diamond from sleeping Bratt's clutches.

BUT IT WASN'T OVER YET.

It turned out that Bratt's acting wasn't as bad as everyone thought. He wasn't knocked out. In fact he was just waiting for an opening , so he could unleash his favourite gadget of all – **HIS KEYTAR!**

A **SONIC WAVE** blasted Gru across the deck and over the side of the ship – that Keytar packed some serious synth.

. . . and passed office blocks packed full of people. Unfortunately, Gru was without his clothes. The Keytar had blasted them off and so the pink bubblegum had not only saved his life, but his modesty too.

He had **NO CLOTHES** and **NO DIGNITY** left, but he did have the gem.

Life was certainly never dull in the Gru household and with Balthazar Bratt on the scene it was only going to get more interesting . . .

. . . because **BALTHAZAR BRATT** was one very bad boy and unlike his TV show, his evil plan wasn't over yet.

Oh, and if you're still wondering about what happened to Dave and Jerry . . . they DJed at the greatest party the beach had ever seen, of course!